Praise for *The Stories of Devil-Girl*

"Anya Achtenberg's *The Stories of Devil-Girl* is a powerful and succinct account of survival. The narrator, who is by turns surrealistic and unflinchingly realistic, recounts her journey from her beginnings in an immigrant NYC Jewish family nearly wiped out by pogroms and by the Holocaust, through her abuse at their hands, her life on the mean streets, and ultimately into a beginning at healing and forgiveness, as she becomes a teacher of others who were victimized, other Devil-Girls. Devil-Girl and those whom she meets along her path, for better or worse — these characters, these voices, are absolutely unforgettable. I wish every teacher would read this book."

> —**Patricia Clark Smith**, Professor Emerita, University of New Mexico; Writer of French Canadian, Irish, and Micmac descent

"*The Stories of Devil-Girl* is a collage of voices weaving birth and death, desire and love, anger and rage, into a powerful spell of words as the speaker 'raves in the road and stops traffic with her stillness.' Rooted in the writer's soul and in Jewish culture, this novella speaks the humanity of us all. By writing in the voice of Devil-Girl, Achtenberg arrives at fresh insights into characters who haunt our daily lives. To come to grips with our warring souls, she shows us 'the difference between prayer and curse.' At times the speaker seems like the devil of disappointment and death; at other moments she is the lyric of prayer. Whether Devil-Girl or Everyman, Achtenberg enlightens us elegantly and eloquently through her gripping work."

—**Preston Hood**, Author of *A Chill I Understand*, Honorable Mention, 2007 Maine Literary Award

"*Devil-Girl's* stories are all of our stories, all of the 'discarded and demonized', all of us who have had to fight to survive, to fight to tell our truths. Achtenberg's wise survivor, Devil-Girl, is witness and seer, and her words are sustenance. There is much pain in this book, much wisdom, and a kind of beauty that sears itself into memory, a fierce beauty that is as necessary as air. Read this book."

—**Lisa D. Chavez**, Poet (*Destruction Bay; In An Angry Season*), and Nonfiction Writer

"Achtenberg is a cutting-edge voice in the literature of the post-globalization age, an era in which we are uprooted geographically and spiritually, and redefining what it means to be home. What a superbly written book! Read it and be changed."

—**Demetria Martinez**, author of *Mother Tongue*

"Stunning and original! Powerful 'make it new' language that creates—through the runaway energy and precise detail of the storytelling voice—a disturbing world in all its particularities, only to transcend it by grappling with what's at stake in the larger world."

    —**Stratis Haviaras**, Founder and former editor
    of *Harvard Review*

"An amazing piece of bravura writing! *Devil-Girl* takes us from destitution to seedy glamour as a homeless vulnerable young woman tries to survive the savagery of the streets of New York. Poignant and fierce, this book is moving, beautifully written, and urgently relevant."

    —**Kathleen Spivack**, Author, and Director:
    Advanced Writing Workshop; Visiting
    Professor of American Literature and
    Creative Writing: Université de Paris, France

About *The Stone of Language*:

"Achtenberg is a poet of lyrical intensity...
interested in detail for the wealth of revelation and music it will yield up."

    —**Luis Francia**, *The Village Voice*

The Stories of
Devil-Girl

by Anya Achtenberg

Reflections of America Series
Modern History Press

Library of Congress Cataloging-in-Publication Data

Achtenberg, Anya.
  The stories of devil-girl / by Anya Achtenberg. -- 1st ed.
     p. cm.
  Includes bibliographical references.
  ISBN-13: 978-1-932690-62-0 (trade paper : alk. paper)
  ISBN-10: 1-932690-62-X (trade paper : alk. paper)
  1. Jewish women--Fiction. 2. Brooklyn (New York, N.Y.)--Fiction. I.
Title.
  PS3551.C418S76 2008
  813'.54--dc22
                                        2008013809

Published by: Modern History Press, an imprint of
Loving Healing Press
5145 Pontiac Trail
Ann Arbor, MI 48105
USA
http://www.LovingHealing.com or
info@LovingHealing.com
Fax +1 734 663 6861

Modern History Press

Reflections of America Series

The Stories of Devil-Girl by Anya Achtenberg

How to Write A Suicide Note: serial essays that saved a woman's life by Sherry Quan Lee

Chinese Blackbird by Sherry Quan Lee

"The *Reflections of America* Series highlights autobiography, fiction, and poetry which express the quest to discover one's context within modern society."

From Modern History Press

The Stories of Devil-Girl

Dedicated to all
who were early discarded, demonized,
and wildly underestimated.

Table of Contents

Introduction

Devil-Girl has been through many incarnations. She has been a double-CD set and is still an MP3 audio file. A nickname for a dear friend's daughter; a candy bar discovered long after Devil-Girl had named herself in my head; and, after going a million miles away to the other side of the mirror, she is perhaps being reborn in Devi Mau, the central character of *History Artist*, a novel-still-in-progress as of the date of this publication of *The Stories of Devil-Girl*.

As various people would question my racial/ethnic "identity", even to the point of the bluntest question presented in the sweetest tones, "What are you, dear?", so may readers question this small volume, looking for its identity in its genre. Looks like prose, sounds like poetry, at least, some of the time. Reads like a fable, but smacks of the truth. Just as I would respond to the question about my identity with a simple, "It's all true," so would I admit the mixed identity of *The Stories of Devil-Girl* with a nod to the way that history must not be buried or allowed to remain the food of amnesiacs. While it can be a challenge to keep track of the truth, I must offer this so-called novella as a true hybrid that aims with its lies and its music only for the edge of truth, and its ability to cut. Cut through, cut away, cut into.

The writing of this novella was much longer than the volume is, and moved with me from my main writerly occupation as a poet into my obsession with storytelling in prose. It took along my own story on the journey of the writing and dropped it down an airshaft or into the sea to explode, or to splatter, into fiction. Once mostly poetry, it left the stutter of line breaks that would not tell what I needed to tell.

The Stories of Devil-Girl is prose fiction, with much that is autobiographical, and, as our lives always are, pushed by poetry.

It is, more for me than for the reader, a document and a time capsule, an air bubble, the black box from the crash, the beginning of breath. Lifesaver. It was the release for me into becoming a fiction writer and novelist. It marks for me the letting go of auto-biography, until perhaps some distant moment, and the freeing of my voice into the multiplication of characters who somehow hold the forces that move us. My first memory is that of someone trying to strangle me in my crib, a memory I seem to always have had, reasonable in context. I read, after this novella was mostly complete, of the first woman, Lilith. It is, then, no surprise, but an act of balance to find a voice in Devil-Girl—the demonized speaker who roams the globe not to strangle babes in the crib, but to protect children.

What this novella is for the reader will, of course, vary, but I can only hope that it is a container holding something of use, something to connect to, something that opens up a bit more space for memory and story, for passion for the world. It is in this spirit that I now offer in print *The Stories of Devil-Girl*.

Anya Achtenberg
May 2008

Storytelling

I was born September the first, my entry into the visible world precisely following the month of August, Devil's Month in Bolivia, far away and not so far from New York, an expensive city because there is always the Devil to pay. I was born here as the one I had violated during another lifetime, I'm sure of it. I was born here to walk the avenue between life and death. To fill out the forms of denial. To rave in the road and stop traffic with my stillness, as some do with their anger. To prowl the bootless alleyways, to drink the spoiled fluids of men. To flail beneath the Devil. To sprout breasts in the lunar lots of Bushwick, where the maws of an old Frigidaire caught my friend Penelope and she froze to a fetus, knees to lips, gray fists clenched.

Devil's month, exhausted and febrile, lay down in me, and I wailed a love song to the Devil, that dapper demon, as I fell from the clutch of my mother's thighs and she waved me away, and something invisible scooped me up and kissed me on one baby nipple, then bit it hard, as I bleated and bucked and shivered in the whiteness of the hospital corridor, fleeing dark as a stain on the Maimonides sheet.

Actually, as I recall, we never made it to the hospital. I couldn't wait, and had for some time been having nightmares of forceps sliding around my tufted skull and squeezing me past thought, or, if not that far, just into the land of deformity. I lived with that nightmare for the last month of my float, and came up pigeon-toed and anxious.

Because of the circumstances and moment of my birth in a speeding taxicab on the evening of the Devil's retreat to gather up force for his next spree, and because of my furious race to be severed from my mother after the nightmare of strangulation I slept with all those months, because of my flight, then, from my origins, my howl moved through all parts of the city, and returned to each neighborhood as I searched for the word my mother said to my first ear at the moment I slipped into hearing the solid world. Repelled so far from the welcoming word and the breast of life, my body was able to measure distance in units of hunger and fear.

Now, understand this, it was because of the silence that spoke in me, because of the daily stories that fed me through the window and the mountainous decay of events in each room that waited for a teller loud enough to be heard, that I have the ability to tell a story. It was because of playing at life in my mind, because of how things shattered, and because of hands. It was because my screams always gave me something to cry about, something to hide and seek. And it was because words also fly away from their origins, and in their dream lives continue to search for them in unbearable whisperings, that I possess the ability to read a man according to his reactions to my storytelling.

Soon, I could measure the distance between a man and his soul, as well as the speed of his flight away from it, by the strength of his punch and the angle at which his knee jabbed into the softest part of my thigh. If he could finish a rape, the taking or the buying peppered with a beating, after a story from my collection, I judged that he had journeyed too far from his soul to ever return home. I soon realized that, for some, a good story only helped to push a rape along. But it was only after a certain someone, a solid businessman with three kids, hurled me through the air into the wall, that I fully understood the power of the word and the limits of matter.

Pretending that I'd never had a mother, I told him a story of myself as a little girl who suddenly appeared in a lively neighborhood uptown with absolutely no memory of a home or parents. I depicted my arrival as a remarkable event, but one with no history. I began to speculate on the route of my entry into girlhood, and on the invisible world that rubs up against the one we can see, from which, perhaps, that girlchild had come. He had no interest in talking spirit talk, and while a man's silence sometimes stopped my words, at other times it set my old tongue wagging with stories. I began to tale him, rapidly. This new child, I said, wandered from tenement to tenement, taken in by families from everywhere, a Black family from North Carolina who watched over me fiercely, a Puerto Rican family who surrounded me with questions and with children who matched me story for story, a Jamaican family who taught me secret language, an old Russian couple who hugged me and wept, on and on, the list drove the fellow crazy. He didn't want to believe me, but he began to enter the weave of the fabric I spun, and could see in my Devil eyes and wild hair that this might all be true. He put his mouth to my ear, but I switched and put mine to his, to whisper more tales.

I described myself to him like this, having read it in Mary Shelley's *Frankenstein* and remembering it always: "...unnatural, bereft of a determinable childhood...no father had watched my infant days, no mother had blessed me with smiles and caresses." I began to weep piteously, my eyes parted to slits to see what the businessman would do.

He was like a dead man, soul flown, no fingers of light. His words: the husks of cockroaches, pomegranate seeds sucked bloodless, wisps of breath through the broken flute. Tears called up no kindness from him. He took my clothes and made me cry for real. It's true, I protested, I did wander the streets, motherless.

I hit the wall, the way the kids next door to us in the projects hit the foyer wall, one, two, three, when their father had been drinking. Infants I might have had flew forth from me, and I slid down the wall, shaking off generations, born again into the streets.

Mother and Child

"When the flame turns around, she rushes off and again goes roaming all over the world to seek out the children who deserve to be punished. And she smiles at them and kills them...."
On Lilith, from *Zohar: The Book of Splendor*,
by Spanish kabbalist Moses de Leon)

Now, even before I find the streets and dirty myself with the crass comings and goings of various sectors of the populace who hope to purify themselves in a shower of Devil's dollars, even before I meet hands that without kindness survey my expanse and jab in the flag of ownership that unclaimed children hunt for, even if accompanied by a new world of pain, I am found to be unclean and in need of daily purification.

Mama is a hard worker, and, no doubt disturbed by the presence of the Devil's hand in my beginnings, seeks a cleanliness beyond reproach in me, her smallest daughter. Let me paint a picture of the ritual: water runs into the tub and she crawls over the tiles, bare arms reaching over the cold white ledge, scouring and cursing, hair unpinned, each stain shed from the body calling, steam rising, flesh shaking, while I sit, not yet four years old, pants at my ankles, suspended over distance, chill and porcelain. She rises up onto one foot, then the other, throws down sponge and powder, spilling a dizzy stream of white, digs her hands into the small of her back and curves over, blouse half opened, hair coiling into the air, breasts lifting up from her soft, marked belly, eyes absent from the steamy cubicle, from the harsh disinfectant, from me.

I sit, trapped by the pants twisted at my ankles. When she sees me looking at her, her hands grow strong and red and she sets to work upon me, rips at my hair, pulls me down by my legs, and it is clear this day that she is not my mother, though I recall the distant view of her inside thighs rushing past me before the thud of birth. I lie on the cold tiles and try to stop breathing until she gets tired, smoothes down the coiling hair which I have also, buttons up the old white blouse against her long and pointed breasts. But I can't be still, so I run into the hallway, my own smells still clinging.

Oh, let me tell you, it gets worse when she catches me...the hottest water, the roughest cloth, some disinfectant...when she holds me down and opens me up and scours and scrapes, the muscles in her arms tightening, sweat running down between her breasts, her curses whispered now. "You devil," she hisses into me, low, and stops my screams in a towel, leaves the neighbors at peace.

Well, you don't have to hit me over the head for me to figure it out, to guess the guilty party who tried to kill me in my crib, who pulls up the blanket of darkness and crushes it around my throat. Nighty-night.

I know I am in danger. And I know to keep my mouth shut. I see that storytelling's an art reserved for future use. I know I must locate the exact middle of night and hunker down there, silent as a tic.

But here's how I tell the story in my head, since I have no other way to say it on such nights.

I call it, "Cleaning":

My best friend is Paulette. Her name's so French, but her great, great grandmother was a slave in a place called Down South. Paulette has lots of grandmothers, some with more greats than others, that go like a necklace of beads of many colors trailing up the map of the United States to Bedford Stuyvesant, then to the projects. Oh, I have only one grandmother, and I remember once I had a great one, but her eyes were like the holes in the gray scrapey concrete for the metal fence poles that keep us off the grass, and nothing was in them, and nothing covered them.

One of Paulette's grandmothers lives with her, and stays home with her when her mother puts on high-heeled shoes and perfume like the honeysuckle I used to bite the ends off and drink, before my mother caught me and beat me because, she said, they put poison on the flowers to kill the bugs. But I didn't taste any poison, just the sweetest drops that stayed in the little lines of my tongue till I put my head back and they kissed my throat and I swallowed.

9

Paulette told me that this grandmother is a cleaning lady and works, most days, in two different houses from six in the morning until midnight. Then she stands in the middle of the kitchen with a big bowl of rice and beans in the crook of her arm, heavier than we can lift, and eats with a tablespoon, cracking each mouthful like a nut. Paulette says it's a joke around the house that as good a cleaning lady as she is, she cleans her plate better than anything else.

My mother is a good cleaning lady, too. My mother uses very hot water, she's not afraid to be burnt. My mother uses steel wool, she's not afraid of getting scratched. She says disinfectant cleans things no one else can see, but the smell makes me dizzy, and my head throbs like I just had a cup of it to drink. When my mother bathes me, I feel it in my teeth. When she scours, the stinging crawls all over my skin and the heat makes me fall like a sack underwater, but my mother is not afraid. "Dirty girl," she says, "dirty girl."

So sometimes I run off to Paulette's apartment and her grandmother tells me stories of the string of beautiful beads journeying to Brooklyn. No one's ever told me stories of so many grandmothers, and when I finally go home, my mother knows where I've been, and she starts cleaning and I could drown, but I don't care, and I tell her so, I don't care.

Mother and Father

Always the dirty child with the Devil in me, I watch to see this first man, first woman, in their thrashings. I listen for their words of anger. I look for what is empty in each to ascertain who has come from whom. I also look for their jaggedness, and study from beneath the furniture to see if the jigsawed edge of her fits his own, and how precisely. I watch the crumbs falling, the hesitant feet, the slipping to the ground of overcoats and dresses, the strange impossible meetings in the nights of darkness I can see through.

I remember once, he cries out. He is choking. And she beats against him, raising her body in a cry of knowledge that stirs the branches outside to strike the window, to enter the room. What does she see when he is inside her? He does not mean to know her or to show himself, little refugee, only to hide for a while, to forget his smallness, to find a place where he would not be hunted. The breasts that fill me with terror would be his sea, his voyage to liberty; the smells she tries to annihilate—the perfumes that call him to climb up out of himself and his brown suits and frayed shirts, out of his slow journeys to the uptown yards where the snakes of subways couple and uncouple and lay their long shining bodies against each other, waiting for him to run his hands over them and know what is missing or needs repair—a light gone dead, a door that will not open, a strap split apart in constant use by hands that clutch and finger it, in the danger and swaying, in the dreaming of the ride. He has not meant to show her anything at all, but whatever it is she sees horrifies her, and she will never again let him rub her roundness, she will never be wet, never let her breasts fall over his chest as she sits above him and comes to him in the waves of the sea.

The sea drains away into the darkness, and I fit precisely into the dry space between the first man and the first woman, hungry, invisible, holy bread swelling in fear and collapsing into smallness each time one of them strikes at the other through my body, red-eyed trembling child. Papa, too, becomes smaller, and walks at night. She no longer looks into his eyes, except years of heart attacks later to search for signs of life. Mama is the word now for absence and anger, the abrupt flash of a gathering storm, the thunderclap that follows the light.

My neck grows out from my hunched body, quite slender above the captive earth, and rough hands measure it, ready to snap it like a dead branch.

I do not yet know what is beginning.

Curse

Of course, early childhood is a time of firsts, a bright season of introduction to what grown people take for granted. And, as most adults know, the excitement of beginnings, of new things, must be balanced with a steady and comfortable routine so that a child feels secure. Now, I'm not bragging, but my Mama is clear about all this. She is reliable. I know what to expect. And, she is in touch with a higher power.

I know this because Mama calls on God when I'm bad. She tells Him exactly what's to be done. My mother knows, and I have been taught, that it was this God that spilled us here, like canned beans into the fry pan, at the edge of Brooklyn, near the miles of warehouses with their guardian gangs of dogs, from out of the *shtetls* in what they call the old, old country. This is a wrathful God, but, if you say so, he'll whup your little bottom and whack you upside the head. So, when my mother clutches at the cloth around her pounding chest and raises her eyes to the damp patches on the ceiling, where I guess God lurks, I listen real hard, like when I've just spilled the milk or the orange juice, and I watch to see what happens.

That's when my mother calls directly on God for action. She follows the milk sliding across the floor, or the juice running down my shirt as it makes a road to my pants, and her eyes open wide, like she sees God moving right there in the spill, and then she yells loud to tell Him just what to do. God comes to me in my father's big hands, and in Mama's red ones, and I know He comes to do just as she asks. I guess He thinks that'll make her stop screaming so everyone in the projects can go to sleep or study their mathematics or hear Lucy on the TV make her loud sound that's not like my mother's loud sound.

When my mother calls on God, I know I'm that close to never leaving our little 4A apartment again. No more cheerful little outings, even to the red-bricked public school. My mother prays to God to take me away from her. She tells Him to carry me out in a box. I never saw a box big enough to hold me and my fast-growing bottom, except once when the neighbors got a new refrigerator and left the carton near the trash. I climbed in to see if there was complete black darkness inside. I couldn't see my hands or my feet, though I could see a silvery wavy line, like a feather falling close to the light of the moon, but when my mother peered into the box, her nose sniffing me out in the darkness, as sure as the warehouse hounds, she howled to the streetlamp, "In the name of God, take this Devil away from me!" I knew I had to jump out quick, right out of the box, because it would have been too easy, her prayers could be granted in a God's breath. My sister says Mama can't really get God to carry me away, it's just a curse, but the curse repeats itself in my dreams, and when I wake up, sometimes she's standing over me, ready to slam down the lid.

So I know just what to expect, from Mama and God both, when I am very bad. What I don't know is why, when my mother calls on God, he answers. In synagogue she has to sit upstairs in the balcony, as if she's dirty, too, and the men are the ones doing all the praying down below, in another language.

Well, maybe I'm doing some of the praying, and to show it, I rock back and forth and move my lips with no sound coming out. I raise my eyes to the slit of light shining up there where the roof needs fixing. I let my breath hum the notes of the black skullcaps way below. I know I must be one of them, one black note in God's house. This is how I pray, but then I just get to thinking, trying to figure out the difference between a prayer and a curse, and which is the more reliable.

I do not think anyone will pray for me. I guess I'd better learn how.

Prayer

Though I am now officially full of the Devil, I still don't think that I'm beyond redemption, and I keep my affection for going to the old synagogue at the end of the Avenue, where the streets are still dirt. The lights in the entryway flicker with bad wiring, and the women ascend their own staircase in darkness, hoisting themselves and their girl-children up with the banister's help.

Once up in the balcony, I want to pray. I sit at the edge of the bench and hang my arms over the worn wood of the railing. My mother keeps flinging my arms back into my lap. I watch the skullcaps bob up and down. I want to feel the bite of the leather straps of the *tefilin* around my arms. I want the fringes of the prayer shawl to dance prettily around me. I want to pray, to call upon God to deliver me. I want the words to fill my mouth, I want the first languages, I want to speak to God and to no one else, none to overhear, none to report, so I make a small drone into the well of my stomach until I can see, spinning into my sight, the pleasures of my few years on this planet: dancing in small rooms, filling with sky, singing beneath a shady tree, wild blueberries ringing into the metal coffee can, stories of flying and of children who escape from law and punishment, rising and falling back with the painted horse of the carousel, legs wrapped tightly around the glowing body.

I drone on, rocking back and forth, counting off my list of pleasures, my heart strong in the darkness, strong among the women who are not allowed to pray, whose voices cannot reach God.

I begin to laugh, and my mother squeezes my thigh with her red hands, breaks the skin with her sharp nails, and when I keep on laughing, not exactly like a little girl, she slaps my face and my laughter leaves me there in the balcony, dizzy over the prayers of men and the sour tales of women, who will not be counted and cannot talk to God.

The Birthday Girl's Requests

I am the Devil's child and the food of Eden on earth
sticks in my craw. So, special day or not, don't stuff
my throat with pink cotton candy, swirled to the
consistency of an old man's beard in the tornadic
winds of the candy machine bearing down with its
rattling wheels on the work of ants. I'm already
through with childish things. Don't throw me a ball
with red and yellow stars on its galactic belly; I'll
pierce it with a look, I'll deflate it with the edge of the
moon of my pinky nail. Don't swathe me in fuzzy
pajamas with bunnies cavorting over my baby fat; I
know what that leads to. And, for the sake of your
health, to avoid my child's ire, my nighttime
eruptions, my experiments with explosives, my
carefully framed leaks of tales you told about the
neighbors and the co-workers, don't send me one of
those birthday cards with my age in gigantic red type,
as if I'm blind as well as captive in this refugee New
World soap opera. No green peas, no board games, no
throwing the ball around, and no kitties, except violent
ones, tiger-striped. The insect world is a comfort.
Birds, yes; fou-fou dogs, no; standard suburban
Lassies running the chained-in green draw my spit,
and can only bark and paw at the accident I've been
in; Rin-tin-tin has a name I can dance to, but German
shepherds are reminiscent of forced flight, so, please,

toss the stick to a mixed mutt with a wise face and a shadowy heritage or Rover might not make it to my next birthday.

And, today, on my special day, surrounded by my nuclear family, let me answer your questions. Genealogy? A death sentence: cancer, heart disease, diabetes, inverted wombs. And sisterhood? Not beautiful. She's threatening blood because it's my day. I am the malformed urchin foil for her, the large pink version named for a Catholic saint in the confusion of arrival in the New World, the one who draws boys like piglets to pudding.

I am gender-troublesome, too smart, too silent, too dark, and capable of storms only heavy hands can harness. Which reminds me, no little drummer boy drums, please, in case you were thinking of a gift. I've been drummed on myself, and I have compassion, at least, for the stretched skin targeted by hands and sticks. Give me a book instead, and forget where you put me, or I'll write a curse especially for you down on the baseboard in print so small you'll go to your grave in a blind convulsion of ignorance.

So, you think I don't know my place? I do. The bare branches are my home and my mirror, my Devil's claws reaching for the sky.

Well, now, let's get to the celebration. Cupcakes with my age on them in pink icing? Creamed corn instead of peas? Spaghetti instead of tuna? I know what's on the menu. Nothing special for my birthday. The menu in the projects is usually the same, except for the occasional show-off holiday meal. But I am a fussy little eater, they all think. After every holiday dinner, the fish I will not eat swims to me and gives me his glistening belly, his salt blood, his fins of angelic translucence, shows me the waves pulled from the ocean's heart, the hope for the top. Sometimes they force me, though I yowl like a sacrifice. The lamb bleeds, the meat is given, the cries forgotten, but I taste the bloody carcass for days, sleep curled around the flayed back beneath the swaying bodies, feet sticky with it in dreams, the sound louder as the bloody walker comes up to my bed, my little neck so easy, blood in my nostrils, snapped branches.

"Eat," they're chanting. "Eat."

Falling in Love

So why does Mary's Frankie sit in his rusted out Ford convertible, parked at the side street near the old library, with the top down and his bottoms off? Marlon Brando undershirt. Tough black curls in his armpits. Five o'clock shadow full out at three-fifteen when I have to walk past to get some books for my assignments. Staring up at the trees while he casually leans over to push the door open for me.

First time, I scream and run past the churchyard and the old crumbly tombstones. His looks fat like a salami, even resting there on his white leg among the black hairs. I'm not in touch with my Devil nature that day, what with the shock of it, but the next time I figure to walk straight into the front seat, oxford heel to oxford toe, and curl up there in his lap. I want to bite it, it resembles so much what sits and hardens in the brightly-lit window of Schneiderman's Deli.

And, like many children, I'm tired of running from the hands and fists of those who act as if their asses are covered. So, as I hope Frankie will soon learn, I plot, I vow, I pray for a street empty of spectators, and a clear path for running away.

The Brighton Beach Flasher has already done his work on me, walked by me like a normal at the beach, where I used to sit dumb to the world of salamis and ripe fruit and thirsty roses opening their petals to drink the world. God, I've been a naïf, barely rushed through the museum of naked women and clothed men to see a pair of breasts other than the ones my mother stuffs into her rocket-shaped brassieres. The BB Flasher does what they call making eye contact, though one eye wanders off, and reveals the little worm living in his pants with a quick rush of cloth down his dry thighs. Then, *pièce de la résistance*, as I later learn to call these supreme efforts, he turns and runs with his pants around his ankles and his baggy buttocks hanging down the backs of his thighs. He looks back at me to make sure I am looking, and hoots and runs and hoots and runs, leaving a trail in the sand that the ocean later washes away.

So I am ready. Lots of preparation. Cheap Charley smacks me on the backside each day when I run to buy his sugar buttons stuck on long rolls of paper, or the candy lipstick I smear up and back over my lips and then lick off, or tootsie rolls I eat section by section after softening the whole thing in my mouth. He keeps the candy in a baby carriage my mother insists has cockroaches in it. If she finds out I shop there, it will make Charley's work look like lovetaps. I guess they are, but by the end of the day, my whole behind is red, and the candy has given me a stomach ache. My lips stay red, too, for another day or more, and so I am ready to go check out Mary's Frankie in his convertible. My teeth are sharp, having gnawed on some chicken bones for the whole week before, as anyone in training might do, but I have to now, if I ever want to get up from the supper table without another scene and a further lesson on the power of hands and the color red.

It's not that I want to destroy Frankie's symmetry, bite off the one and the two of his nether regions, it's just that I want him to know that it can be done, that greater towers of power are cloaked in wait, that firestorms can be unleashed over East New York and beyond. I just want him to know, as he lingers bare-assed in convertible comfort, his tail lights spurting red under his command, that his game on the side streets of Brooklyn, his planting fear or worse in the insides of little girls, will be multiplied and explode when children step on landmines to the tune of losing their feet, their arms, their eyes, on the road to school, to the store, on their way home. The news talks about it. There are bombs aimed every which way right now. I just want him to know, as he bends some young girl to his drama and his weeping eye and his weakening, that there are assembly lines of spurts that aren't only for girls, that bury all.

But back to this girl, me, and all these men uncovering themselves at the sight of my sweet Devil mouth and incipient bosom and burgeoning buttocks. Still, it is the man in Manhattan who covers himself with sandwich boards of impenetrable wood and messages about the end of the world who captures me, my imagination, and the tingles at a place way inside me.

I wonder how it breathes beneath his messages, if it finds a way to grow when it has to, if anyone gets invited to look at it, or if he simply keeps it to himself, more concerned with the important business at hand than with the little worm, as his beard grows down toward his feet and wraps me in the mystery of prophecy and the wonder of wooden clothing that makes him look like a life-size playing card, or a god.

He hurls his words like a rock that gets heavier as it falls. "The end is near."

I always thought so, too.

His voice gets low and he closes his eyes.

I close mine, too.

Lesson in the Elevator at A&S

"....Did he smile his work to see?
Did he who made the lamb make thee?

Tyger, Tyger burning bright,
In the forests of the night:
What immortal hand or eye,
Dare frame thy fearful symmetry?"

"The Tyger" from *Songs of Innocence
and of Experience* by William Blake

Did they who made the lamb make me, in all my
fearful symmetry? Is this why I am growing meek,
meeker with every birthday? Cast out of the
synagogue's balcony, a curse in the kitchen, blows
with dinner, force-fed my animal sisters, my fishhead
brothers, interrogated in middle school, graded on
each breath. In what dread furnace burns my brain,
beneath the sizzling rush of rain? They ask me, in
speech and on paper, "What are the economic,
political and social causes of World War I? Just repeat
what the fat yellow book says," they harp. My breath
comes fast at these questions, my heart jumps to the
tune of grenade, my eyes won't blink and I fail, daily,
in utterance, when this litany comes to me: the causes
are your greed, the causes are your ugliness, the
causes are the stealth of your step over us, the causes
are the boot salesmen and the bullet manufacturers,
the land grabbers and the army song singers; and the

poor flattened Archduke and the little Devil-Boy who killed him are only pageant, and you're asking me? You're asking me? Put down in my notebook the causes of war? I am a child, thirteen years old. In the city of the night. I have only the words of a child. If you want three causes, I will give you three causes, and they are you, you, you. Now, I know there are more numbers than one, two, three, because Shirley's mother has nines and sevens among the numbers on her arm, and so does her father, and there are zeroes everywhere at the end of casualty lists where people disappear into approximations, and a ninety-nine at the end of every price, and, most of all—ten, there are ten fingers held against the mouths of people I pass, as they lift their two hands in some kind of shock and they see the cause, the cause of it all. I'm the cause of it all, their gasp says—me, Devil-Girl—and the twist in my face is the war map, the target drawn all along the bone.

Bark at me, boys, bark at me, and they do. Lanky or thick, stunted or stretched, Italian, Black, Jew, Irish, Puerto Rican, they lean, with their hints of beards, their hints of tough, their throats popping with harsh, unpredictable highs and lows.

They lean in wait and when I pass, twisted history map, they bark at me, o holy besmirched child of broken cups, and, at night, howl harsh, howl into laughter, score the glass of my heart with their blades.

Brillo, they call out, as my hair coils into the afternoon, and that night I dream they use me that way. Though I'm not pink like soap, but yellow. My big pink sister bats her eyelashes at me and sweeps past. My striped polo shirt is swelling, and sooner or later my yellow body, my hint of Mongolian breasts, yellow to the girl nipples, needs a change of clothes.

Just once, I remember to pray, new ones, just once, no hand-me-down, hem-ragged, button-popped Halloween schoolgirl outfit.

So for once my prayer is answered and my father takes me off to downtown Brooklyn. There's a crowd in the elevator. No air. I'm gasping. My father's beside me, above me, silent. The man behind me rubs against the deep wall of the magical ride, as we fall between heaven and the marketplace. His shoulders frame his proud chest. How do I know this? Where are my eyes?

I can't see him. I just know his back's not bowed. He's not the one who'll have to apologize for crying out. I am.

The lady in the girls' department tells my father I'm tall like a model, but he grimaces at my gawky looks, my wiry hair, the groaning angles of my face. She smoothes the cloth down over my hips. He turns away, wanting beauty.

I see his face when the dressing room lady eases open the fitting room curtain and I step resplendent for a moment into his judgment, his immigrant shame.

My immigrant bones and awkward flesh, my iron wool hair and homeless eyes, meet his tired stare and his gesture, "If that's the best you can do."

The bag, a badge of ugliness, a sack of hope, swings. I want to believe, the right light, my hair straight, the magic of the cloth can cover me. If no one wants me the way I am, I'll show them, I threaten, and clutch the neck of the bag tighter, knowing my new outfit sways there like a pendulum of love, towards me and away, towards the new swell of hip and breast, away from my startled hair, its smell of pomade, away from my teeth, away from the silent nipple of my tongue.

He'll take me home now. The elevator opens to swallow us. The mirror above watches us stand on our heads, legs waving in darkness. Shoppers crowd in, flesh to flesh, purchases pressed to thighs and chests, hair spreading against the mirrored ceiling, skirts falling away above. The man behind me, with his claws and angry beak, his hungry beak, scoops my flesh, bends into places tender with not knowing, his own little worm dying for moist ground, for home. I'm trapped here, howling, lodged in the crowd. My father, quiet, stares straight ahead, but that awful bird is hot in my ear, cawing and gouging as if I were dead tiger sprawled with cheek to the hot forest floor, flanks exposed, paws folding to death, while the center of me, still fevered with life, throbs with blood. The bird rips and sucks.

I learn again to be the kill. I learn again my paws are all, my roar, my fury, all an orphaned tiger has against the birds of prey. I burst out, the crowd annoyed, shaking their heads, "She must be crazy!" My father locks my arm in his grip and hisses, "What is wrong with you?"

He drags me off and I try to tell about the man behind me in the mirror above. I learn again that fury is all an orphaned tiger has. I learn to hold it in the mirror above my head, my hair spread against it. I learn to step through the curtain with my head down. I learn who my father is, I learn to be dead tiger. I learn what is wrong with me. I learn to let my legs wave in the air, and how I can disappear in the crowd, my father beside the space I leave, his back to me, satisfied with the lesson I learn.

First Try

It is the moon, oh rapture, and his thighs, long and hard, and his breath, hot, enveloping, and the open window darkness streaming in like river water, and his hands, soft and ceaseless, and the perfumes, ours and the night's, in his house, a real house under trees, his parents gone, and his cries in the night and our marching together for peace and our anger and my blue and white dress with its flowers I will never see again, and the car ride, the wind, his hand, my thigh, the kisses, the promise that I can dream myself out of ugliness. I live there before that window under the moonlight, eating hungrily, hands and mouths, clothing slipping down into the field of night, his eyelids, the swooning, my god my breath the climbing the motion and I begin opening

but I can't. The work of the past is done. God blessed the scoured blossom of my Devil-Girl mound with bloody fear. Father blessed it, pounding. Mother blessed it, screaming. Sister blessed it, smirking. Boys blessed it with their violence and their laughter. Strangers drank it. Doctors probed it. Dogs nuzzled it. Heart ran from it. Someday, money will bless it and take it to the bank. But joy will not find it for a long time, and the boy with long thighs and peach tongue hurls himself from a rooftop in despair over the bombing of Cambodia.

Coffee and Wine

Wolf girl, I run to the wild, and take my howl with me. My fangs push out, ready for animal or vegetable. Shocker, after my urgent prayers for liberation from the silent bloodletting, for myself and the creatures around me, but I start to wax nostalgic for the old family suppers with their clatter of tin cans and their multi-purpose utensils to stir, to poke, to jab and to test. But the food was, after all, edible, and maybe the way it got stuck in the epiglottis of speech had little to do with the seasoning. Too late. I'm gone, hidden in memory, and the friendly chats at our family dining table are a thing of the past. Now I am under cafeteria tables and burger stand stools, hunting scraps, howling belly hunger and cutting my eyes at anyone chewing a sandwich in public. Soup's become the sea of desire; finding a stray pack of oyster crackers, hitting the jackpot.

For a while there's a soup kitchen on the west side, beyond the meat packing plants. Their blood-stained work coats flying, the men who guard the swaying carcasses offer their hammy touch and I think, just sometimes, sustenance there for the licking, but their boots are stuck in the congealed fat of butchered animals, and I run off into the west towards the gray river before I become rump roast, to get on line for stale soup, rotten greens, hard bread.

I learn the price of food, and, sometimes, though perhaps still unsullied by some standards, think I might do it for a candy bar. Oh, Lord of Wine, your bacchanalia is appealing to the well fed, but me? I fall at the feet of the mother of the fertile horn, the cornucopia flowing with grains and fruits, with fish and fowl, dear dead hung neck birds. I worship the mother of beans, the father of crackers, the goddess of jelly, the god's jar of peanut butter. I would do it for a burrito. I would all but do it for a tuna fish sandwich. I would open to tongues for a Reese's peanut butter cup, I would dance nude for a pizza. I would stuff it all into my mouth for a real sausage.

After the soup kitchen closes down, I go on a daily prowl for food. I buy a coffee and sit hoping for a stab at someone's leftovers. I wait for the leaving, eyes focused in stalk, and only at first carefully cut off the contaminated edges before I push the rest into my mouth and my pockets.

The city is a hunt: a sit, a bite, a newspaper, a place to sleep, even if half upright. It's a sweater in the trash, an old pair of tennis shoes. I offer in return a curse for the rain, a rage at the cold, a dead rage shivering at the bookstore stalls. I stretch out that cup of coffee, its arc from lips to saucer and back, like the slow cry of a wounded bird falling to sea, and its spirit rising back up. Then I watch the cup trembling in its saucer like a once-spinning top, there, in the corner of a child's bedroom, before it falls. I see the light leaving me, falling into the devouring twilight sky through the streaked shop window. I lose streets. I lose names. I lose the land of upright. I who might have been the little princess of penmanship lose writing as I shake with hunger, pen in my empty hand.

This late afternoon, I don't even know where I am. I meet him over the empty porcelain cup, lined and greasy, I'm staring into. He speaks to me from a dream, I watch his lips move. My fingers drum the Formica, my eyes close in moisture. He speaks in the heavy accent of his country, and I answer, after a while, with the hard crust of city I chew.

His hair is like mine, dark and curling, but his skin like chalk, his eyes strangely blue. He buys me a sandwich, and I chew each bite until I can drink its memory. He tells me stories of Israel, and of battle. "We can't rely on anyone else, we can't allow others to have power in our own country. We will be our own masters," he says, holding my hand tightly. The talk makes me tense. I argue, but he pounds the table and raises his voice, "I'm the one, you know? I'm one of those who will save the land so your ungrateful little Jewish ass will have a place to sit down! I have done, as always, what had to be done, and you? Look at you. Making a meal of a cup of coffee!"

"Some bad luck," I tell him, "that's all."

"Really," he stares at me, "and where is your family? Where is your home?"

When I am silent, he asks again, but then the silence inside me roars until hearing is no more.

He calms down and reaches for my hair across the table, twirling a bit of it around an index finger, then slides the finger down to trace and retrace my collarbone. "It's Jews like you," he leans over and whispers, "who break our hearts. We are alone in this world, and we've got to take care of our own."

We leave the coffee shop and walk many blocks into an orthodox neighborhood. No Jewish girls like me, wild hair and rough-dressed, no Devil-Girls like me. Wig-decked women with carriages. Neat girls, scrubbed, with brothers playing under *yarmulkas* and *paith*. No ecstatic dance to God. Long black coats limp over commerce. Dusty Talmuds for sale. Empty candlestick holders. Hebrew and Yiddish and the English of small children ring out past fragrant bakeries. Rolls of dark fabric lean against dim cool windows. Bloodless chickens hang, shorn of feathers and their own song. I see men mill about in front of the *shul*, counting themselves into a *minyan* of ten for prayer. No one calls out to me.

He holds my arm, and when someone greets him, he nods and pushes me down the street faster. Then he stops and unlocks a glass door, and I see my face swing into the darkness. We walk up four flights of slanting wood stairs. He opens the door to his room and we are alone.

We drink wine, sweet and red, and I think of Passover and my drunk cousin and the beginnings of drunkenness in my own blood. He fills my glass again. One moment follows the other without warning, no crossing of the room. One moment he watches me drink. The next comes with his hands, and the next with his heaviness upon me.

I am the fool, wine in my teeth. He thinks he's better. "A real Jew, I am," he says, trembling, "who speaks the real language of Jews!" He hisses in my ear the old curses of the Bible: "Whore of Babylon, Lilith, destructress!"

Something dying has whitened his hands; he slaps me, and then he slaps me harder for the things I said. He strikes me with his fists, and the men stand in front of the *shul* below, counting themselves, afraid to dance anymore. He shakes me like a rattle and my hair flies, yes, like snakes, around my thin neck.

I try to slide out from under him, but he grips my wrists in the vise of his white hands, and leans in on me with all his weight. "I know you," I whisper to him. "I know who you are," I say, and he strikes me again and again. "I am different, and I'll prove it to you," he tells me, and his invasion frees me from the wig and the balcony, and the ten men and the cleansing bath that was waiting for me, and I bleed full on his sheets, and smear the blood on his cheek, on his white hands.

He finally sleeps, but the door is locked from inside with his hidden key. I scream out from the window, but only once before he jumps up and makes me be quiet. The men are inside the shul now, repeating each other's low prayers, their women fussing over the Sabbath table. The coffee and the wine both sting the pit of my stomach, and I crouch in the dark corner until he lets me out, a curse on his lips.

I find a quiet street and sit on the stoop in the night air. The light brings me to another coffee shop, where I drink the morning black. I use the restroom, propping one foot against the door with its broken lock, to wash the dried blood from my thighs. I make a call at the corner booth, but no one answers.

The ceremony is over.

Only God knows it is done, and the two of us. Only I will remember.

Pictures

There are things that even I can't say, Devil-mouth, Devil-tongue, from the dictionary of barb and heat and nakedness. Born in a cab, but I can't get one these days. My harpy cry of "Taxi!" falls flat, as if being born once — in the big old Checker — were enough. One look at my costume, and most know I'm no paying customer. Pouches of pockets swaying open with shadow. Soles of my shoes racing to catch up with my stride. Others raise one arm and the journey swings open the door to its sweet center, but all I can do is turn my back and allow the world its ride.

There are so many things I can't say.

But here's one of the rides, along one of the streets of lost notes, up the slanting staircase of downtown, during business, during storm, during torrential flood or the gray ice of New York bitterness undressed and thudding against the spine. Here's the arrangement, the contract, the bonework, the rent split open, the sandwich that saves me from death, the things I must drink.

At the top of the elevator shaft, the cage opens its accordion gate and I am here in a red room where men eat well. Here they pound each other's backs in excitement and the breath of vodka slides down their throats while women wait. I am here in this red room and recording, each gesture slow, each bellow caught in the liquid air. I am here.

I am in this picture and holding: poses, breath, heart. I am still hungry, and running to the edges of my skull on the hunt.

The man in the center seat raises his hand and motions for me to come to the couch. I am looking for food: cheese, nuts, bread; I am biting the pink inside of my cheek. My will is gone, the law is his. I do not know this place, nor the other men sitting to each side of him, but I know the law. I have been taught the costs of lawlessness. Four faces are around him: lion, goat, bull and bird, thick and furred, sharp and fluttering. Light falls on them only, none falls on me. No one can find me here, no one here would hide me.

He has a round face, smooth and lax, and grips a drink in one fist. A cigarette burns from a deep red ashtray. He gestures for me to sit in front of him on the edge of the coffee table. George sits to his left; he is the man who finds me wandering downtown, weak from hunger. He is the one, sharp-featured, constantly blinking, moist eyes, nervous hands, who hooks his arm into mine as I cross Seventeenth Street, aiming for the park to rest. He steers me into a restaurant and watches as I eat, trembling, the sandwich and soup the waitress in pink arranges on the placemat. The warmth of day rises in me with the warm soup and coffee, which I sweeten luxuriously and hold in my teeth before each swallow.

He lays a hand on my thigh, runs a finger around the lens of the camera that hangs from his neck, and smiles at me. His words quiet into breath, breath in my ear and warmth at the base of my spine. You are beautiful, he murmurs (I can see my pink sister crack a rib at that one), and I need beauty, he says. It will be fine, safe and quiet, just a few pictures, a nice fee.

The others leave, though I can hear their voices in the next room. George tells me exactly what to do. Each flash of light fixes me somewhere, a card to be played. With each flash my blindness grows, and George darts out from behind the camera to push me back against the sofa, legs open, or to raise my arms, the fingers of one hand around the other wrist. He tells me to move, I move. He tells me what to think of, as he pushes my own hand between my thighs, and I see all of it: a man above me, where his hands are, what his tongue does, how he rocks into me.

Can you see it? George asks. Can you feel it, the hunger at your breasts, the hard measure of your worth moving inside you? I do as I am told, see and feel as his story urges me. The light flashes like an electric storm, crackling and dangerous, the current's jagged direction pointing me out.

I want to get up now, but I fall into the sweet darkness of the couch, then his hand, then my own, and he says I am beautiful and it is good, the way I lie there, the way I move, how wet I am, how soft, how clean and perfect.

The camera works ceaselessly, the heavens electric, the darkness between moments of captivity on film a blessed bath in which I am released from all that I am in the light.

And when he says he is finished, I fall into the round back of the sofa and drink the darkness.

Work

Devil-Girl is now prowling nights. No food but what the night leaves. No song but the one that glitters in the window of a dark building. Makeup smeared with hunger, blouse open down to the sale items.

Then she hits the last car of the subway heading uptown, and the doors close, taking her to the top of the island to sleep in the Indian caves of Inwood.

Now I'm alone for the night, cursing it, and drink from the bottle like a baby to get ready for my audition, but I cradle the howl from the caves in the center of my ear.

My shoes hit the concrete like dead notes.

When I get there, I press the buzzer and a silent growl shakes the door open. The elevator climbs its cord, then drops to the basement behind me after I step out. Cave of my heart, elevator shaft of my gut, I curse my lips into a smile.

The cigarette is burning to ash. I watch the smoke rush up into the air and disappear. I feel a little dizzy as he explains what I have to do. His voice comes to me from a great distance, though he leans in close to my ear and lays his hands on my knees. He pulls me close to him and handles me, I think, although I forget everything while it is happening. I forget his hands and I forget the hands of the others. I do forget. I can't feel them bruising me and burning me. I forget the look of these men, although sometimes I'll see someone and my heart contracts for longer than a moment, but I can't be sure.

   If I try to remember, it comes to me that I say nothing but yes, but I say yes.

   He sits on the center cushion of the long couch. I see his bare legs extended; they lift me and place me between. I feel a hand like iron at my back, and the world becomes my work between his legs. I feel the others at me. Their boss is groaning. Someone is holding my head until my neck aches in the grip. I hear a terrible sound, from his throat, I think, and he pushes me away. They're upon me then, heavily.

   I hear him laugh. He says things I've heard before, but I realize then that they are about me. He tells the others what to do. They do it, all of it, as if their bodies belong to him, their hands, their organs, their cruelty, their desire. Or perhaps they aren't cruel at all; I am a package there before them, I have been sold. There is nothing they know that can save me. There is nothing I can do. I think I go away, but they continue to take me, and some are laughing, some yelling. They get exactly what they want, each one. I don't remember, but they tell me about it over and over. Cigarette smoke fills my lungs, sweat runs down my brow. I sit on the lap of the man in the center, his fingers inside me, and he tells my future.

I don't recall the day or the season, but it is always warm in that place. There are many photographs of women, and of parts of women, and of things being done to them. I do not care to see them, but he balances them on his lap and forces my head down to look. There are movies of the same things they do to me. The movies never stop, a woman is always falling, someone always above her.

When George brings my first customer, he smiles and says the man is a friend and I should take good care of him. The man starts to take his suit off and tells me to help. He does not look like a man to me, as he is covered with hair, but he does not feel like an animal, his body too rigid and his voice too thin. He tells me what to do. It doesn't help. I lie at the edge of the bed and stare into the dim light in the hanging lamp, hoping, I think, it will burn away something behind my eyes. I am paralyzed and he is losing patience, his money fluttering anxiously on the bare bureau. Then he tells me to call him daddy, and I hold on to him, and he fucks me.

After he leaves, George comes in, takes the money off the bureau and kisses me goodnight.

Search for the No

Fatherless, I roam. Dead-tongued kisses lodged in my throat. O silent mother of the throttled projects, remember me. O father, get off the subway. Mother, stop eating your dry toast. Boys, give me a true hand. Sister of the slap, be kind.

I am a girl made of rags. I am the true crawl, the dead belly, the eye socket of the future. I am the open mouth of forgetting.

I see myself on the corner. I am turned to wood. I am priced on sale. Sip the soup of bile in the coffee shop. I am regarded, not highly. Crush the crackers as I walk, follow the crumbs to the alley where I spill over into rain.

I lie down in it.

If I do not die, I will make a story speak. If the song from the window blesses me. If the siren passes me. If the children do not laugh at me. If my rags do not burn in the darkness. If the night moves by me.

The light now. I must eat.

The howl in my ear is faint, so I ride uptown on a hunt. I circle the rock of Inwood that tells in raised bronze letters of the sale of Manhattan to the Dutch. (The Dutch live now in old church tombstones, in street names. In the one wooden house left standing near Dyckman Street.) But the dream of the hill goes on. Trees tied upright to the clouds, path to the Great Open Ear. Acorns crushed beneath my heel, the bitter meat, my strength. The legend in bronze leaves out the prayer in the cave where I sit, there in the coolness of stone and the comfort of shadow, where an arrowhead pierces the earth littered with broken glass, and my wrists sing out for their own blood.

No, says the light at the mouth of the cave, no, say the leaves in the wind, and the trembling shadows agree.

Then everything speaks, with the light, with the leaves, with the shadows, with my own blood. The ache of the cold in the cave walls. The grit of the rock and the sand and the jagged acorn shells below me. And I keep asking. For deliverance from the body of rags, and from choking.

It is some time after this I think to become a writer, after this, that words become what I desire, what I want to hold in my mouth, hurl at the dogs chasing me, give back hard, gloves off. I decide that I'll become a reporter documenting the lives of abandoned children: an immigrant daughter, a homeless teen, a prostitute, a malnourished kid out on the streets, an underage sexy mama, a saleable object, an honor student gone wrong, an amnesiac, an unemployed youth, a fat girl, an antiwar activist, a race traitor, a disappearance, a shadow on the museum wall, a hush, a turnstile jumper hauled in to the precinct, a potsmoker, a sexually ambiguous runaway in army/navy clothes. And a naked sixteen year-old laying up in the East Village with a man three times her age and a bottle of scotch. A rented house cleaner hunting the upper east side toilets. A clerk on the floor of the backroom with arms bleeding from rusted file drawers and dress torn according to the boss' regulations. A sub-minimum-wage burger flipper, a delivery girl, a waitress, a wolf, a bird, a hammer, a nail, a drowned coat, a broken zipper.

As after any long silence, words accumulate. Words reach for their fellows, their sister sounds, their lovers. They want live births, they rage through labor. It is no different for a Devil-child crying out from under the blanket of night. The words are there. They come to mean everything to a naked army of girl. But then, when no one listens, less than a doorknob, less than the edge of light slanting under the bedroom door.

So where the hell were you, darling words, why didn't you do something, I want to ask. But now, I can take words or leave them. I have bigger fish to fry, other things on my plate, harder nuts to crack. I have work to do on the book of life. I have things better left unsaid. You hear me, words? You know the old song? "...got along without you before I met you, gonna get along without you now...." Well, I'm singing it!

Oh words, boon to my life, orchard of delight, memories of dreams, underwater animals, coral of the mind, war chant and love song, listen to me, and get this right!

There is not a desperate bone left in my body for you, language, little words. You've failed me so many times before that I'm no longer afraid you'll abandon me, leave me like that rough girl, jagged-boned, to swim in a realm of the senses without even the word, no!

You fail me again, but I swim off, and sink, and learn the colors of phosphorescence in the invisible parts of the body. I sink. No rope. Deaf humankind, darkened planet. No word no to stop the slide. Without the no, I die. Without the sound from wound-tight gut, tongue pushed to palate in clear refusal, *no!* I die and die and die, to laughter, to hands, to the knife, the ones that think girl is meat, girl is candy to unwrap, crack and suck sweet syrup, girl is photo to wrap hot limb, to toss with tissue, soiled, torn, silent in the wind at the bottom of the trash.

Where is the no? Where is the word? Where is the sound, the wound wailing, language conjugating its power over and over?

With my softest lick of sound, I know and I remember, that above the blank page all happens, and all the words we have cannot cover that, that naked girl too cold to say no, sinking in the wordless sea.

Marriage Rituals

"Talmudic law established that when a man and woman decide to wed, the man need only say to the woman, in the presence of two witnesses ...that she has now become his wife through one of the accepted forms of marriage—symbolic handing over of money, written guarantee, or sexual intercourse. When the act takes place with the concurrence of both parties, a marriage has occurred." (p. 130)

The Essential Talmud, by Adin Steinsaltz

It is a cold winter, unusually so, and the radiator hisses but remains cold, and my hands stay gloved, and the tea is thin, but I am inside now. I would begin my story, I would stop time with it, I would dance with the darkness into the rhythm of the tale, but the creased page of my burdens remains silent, remains bare, in the holy night of cursing rising from the streets, full of the hiss but not the heat I need to spin.

There is a way to be warm. The old way. The way they pointed to at home but then dropped their arms and abandoned hope at the sight of me. But now, I have been asked. I was pouring coffee and scraping grease, sallow in pink and strapped into apron, writing on green pads and counting change, and I was discovered, and asked.

As with all young women, deviled or not, thoughts turn to marriage. Having been almost married, almost married in stairwells, almost married in backseats, almost married in the balcony of an old Brooklyn movie theater, almost married in an alleyway, and close enough in the park at night before there was a curfew, I say, why not, and look to join my future to another. Having been dressed up, or half-dressed, set on the table, not to sing childish songs, but in the hush of nakedness to display the list of parts in the order called out by the ringmaster, I know that presentation is half the deal, so I work on this, and call my new acquaintance, the one that makes a few bucks arranging marriages.

At the meeting with my potential husband, the Devil makes me dance, and the oscillating fans in the hot Bronx apartment raise each veil until it settles in a heap of nylon on the thick shag rug. I guess I am in a bit of a hurry, being not so much hungry for love, as hungry.

He is older, an East Indian man from the Caribbean who wants very badly to stay here in the United States. He comes to see me in my little room on Ninth Avenue. We agree early on that we will go through with it, and he comes by every few days to drill me on the things I have to be sure of to face Immigration and get through their questions. I have to study a list of the dishes he likes to eat, I have to know what kind of shampoo he uses, what brand of razorblades he shaves with. I have to know what he does at his job, what time he leaves for work, and when he comes home, such things as these. We agree upon the price

— it's more money than I've ever had in my hands, and I am so tired of claustrophobic offices, dingy coffee shops, cold monotonous factories where I sell myself, and unemployment lines when nobody will buy.

We are married in a civil ceremony at City Hall, traces of the chocolates he brought me to clinch the deal still lingering in the corners of my mouth. He holds me up in front of the judge, careful to keep me from swooning with the emotion of the moment, or tripping in the borrowed heels that make me taller than him.

I leave a few things at his place in the Bronx in case someone from Immigration comes to check up on us. After he gives me the money, he starts, I think, to feel like he really does own me, and to tell you the truth, that's kind of a relief. Perhaps, if he owns me, he'll take care of me. His body is thick, he eats well; he feeds me curries and fragrant rice with plenty of wine. The more he feeds me, the more he handles me.

The deal moves along when he pulls me down to sit on his lap. He holds me around my waist with a meaty arm, an arm covered with silken black hair. He gives the shell of my ear his spiced whisper, his constant proposal, his wish to make the paper we have signed vibrate with agreement, and then pushes his thigh up hard between mine.

I know I have already been sold. I don't much care what else happens. He holds me in the heat of his lap for a long time, and it feels good. His fingers are thick and soft, and he reaches for what he has bought. By the dim light thrown inside from the Concourse, he puts the wineglass to my lips. The warmth of the wine spreads as it slips down my throat to where his other hand lies. I can't see his face or understand his distant language; his words are only heat in my ear.

If I remember right, it is then he takes me to bed. It doesn't really matter. He has paid, and that's the way these things work.

I do remember lying on my back next to him, watching his belly rise and fall. I grab the wineglass from the night table and, after a deep swallow, pour the rest down the slopes of my body: red streams, red roads, scars, tracks, incisions, evidence falling onto the sheets. His meaty hands reach for me. I become very still except for the sweet red rivers searching me. I startle him when I take the empty wineglass, smash it on the bare wood floor and grind it to crystals with a bloody shoe, a bloody hand.

Devil-Girl Goes Home

In this long dying as a married woman journeying to the conjugal bed in the Bronx once or twice a week, my so-named husband disappears during a rash of deportations and without so much as a matrimonial smack on the ass. My dying continues. My words choke on dark waves, ride out on purple veins of shells, and hide, gnawing on silence. I move around only at night. And what sights! Meteor showers, storms of serpents plunging through the stratosphere, tails of fire blazing. I follow the gameboard of the city, wheeze along the constellation of smothered infants, pound my head to the beat of the music of pillows dancing on their blue cheeks.

Unemployed again, but I have work to do still, moving over the globe in a nightly ride. I transform myself into stands of trees, where each bruised prostitute can hide from the beating due her because of her sex, or his. No beatings tonight, no beatings. The snakes of my hair wrap the earth in their cool, continuous slither, as if all would wake early into the scent of flowers, the luxurious body of the mother, the shining craft riding us out to sea.

Night after night, I roll around the planet, stalking the marketplace, noting the vendors, whispering to the betrayed. I come to the place of windows or of stalls, where they sell god, sell goddess, sell children, eat the young, spin women into dance till they collapse in their places. I come to where no one is safe, and I know I am at home. Truth is everywhere, hanging, spinning, crawling, stitching, digging, flying, crouching, bearing itself on its own shoulders, swaying its burdens from the top of its head.

I remind the night what is hiding in its folds, and it bears down, and the stories yet unspoken begin to come.

The sun rising here means that child laborers on the other side of the world will see stars through holes in factory roofs above the bricks they bake and haul, while right here the jobless, cradling their worn foreheads in their palms, hunt the want ads in the still dark of morning.

Devil-Girl I am, and not for nothing. I watch them haul my friends off to the joint, one by one, except for the out-of-towners with degrees. One for marijuana, one cigarette's worth. One for picking up a dollar that fell from the pocket of an undercover cop pretending drunkenness. One for robbing a bar after searching three months for work, and refusing to ask his mother for a subway token. One for hooking to get food and diapers for her baby. One for being in the wrong place at the wrong time since birth. One for not speaking English. One for helping me. One for running. One for not running.

One day while I was passing the Women's House of Detention, the screams of the inmates to their families and friends in the street below cut my blood like a knife fallen to dam the red ride, and I know the next thing on my shopping list is a bus ticket out. I'll get out of here if I have to swim, out of the lots and the hallways with my name smeared at the bottom of the wall, as if someone lay forever on the ancient filth ground into the world beneath my back, holding the marker like a knife plunging into the crumbling news left there in passing. I scramble to make some money, careful with my skirt since I'll be traveling and want to make a nice appearance, and get as far as Massachusetts.

The Virgin Mary lifts her stone head as I climb up the stairs behind her to install myself in a room in the boarding house she watches over. The coughing from the tenant next door goes on like machine gun fire, rata-tatting me back to stories of the Second World War, told to me to make sure I would be very, very grateful to be here in America. The Nazis march into town, already a town of ghosts and bloodstains and hidden axes and hoofbeats, breeding photos where the blood remains still as a moment, and rata-tat, or maybe one clear cold shot at a time, my grandfather's sister. Then her daughter. Then her daughter's daughter, a little one with potential for mischief. In front of her father. He's held back by three soldiers, one at each side and one to hold his head up like a dying tree braced by its own last thought, so that he can live out his days watching and helpless until the war's end followed by his suicide.

The family that abandoned me utterly, let me play war orphan in the streets of New York, comes to visit me, files in one by one or in groups arranged by hometown and era to display their silent drama, but spins off into darkness with each new coughing fit from the old woman next door, the pageant's insistent emcee.

I'm up each night, and sleep mostly at twilight, when I don't know whether it's day or night and the ghosts don't either, for though they strain at the edges of the room, they never get clearer than a footstep or a muffled cry at that rupture called dusk. Perhaps it's at that hour they journey in and set up for the nightly performance, but at any rate I catch a couple of hours then and wake up in darkness, check the weather through the jagged lightning of window, and wave to the dim glow of the Virgin who has kept me through my nap, and instructs me on how to turn my body to stone, cold hard robed stone.

It's the night before the grand return to Proskurov, Ukrainian town of my father's childhood, that I learn to step out evenings, under the judgmental eye of the Virgin who'd rather I doze in the windless sweep of her stone cloth, than lean over the bar to request a coffee that will turn to vodka.

A long night. I decide to get to know my surroundings, this new place, first thing next day. I figure it's more of the same. More ice, less noise. I stumble down into the steam of a basement restaurant for an early lunch, Greek music and static from a speaker leaning over the heads of the eaters. Egglemon soup and lots of bread. I hide out in the cloud rising from the bowl. When the waiter brings extra bread, I feel happy, warm and happy.

Later on I stroll with the tourists and the homeless in the Commons, and walk along with the shoppers on Washington Street. I fight for a shirt I can't buy, tugging with indignation over the heaps of clothing on Filene's tables. It's not Brooklyn, not Fulton Street, where record shops one body wide hoist speakers over their doors to blare out James Brown and Marvin Gaye and Aretha Franklin, and the shoppers dance down the street, and across it, and spin into bargains they make look better than the sweatshop owners ever intended. It's not Brooklyn, but the air is cleaner, cold like knives, and suddenly I can see, and there I am in the reflection of the department store window, Devil-hair flying, hands in my pockets. I watch myself make my way, strong against the fierce wind, and pull my collar tighter to my neck to protect myself, as I walk away into the dim winter light shot through by streetlamps. When the door to a music shop swings open as I pass, the strains of a jazz flute caress me and the crowd around me, excited, melodic, going home, nobody after us.

But this is the day I keep turning corners and it seems I run into a crowd that has other intentions. I am walking at a casual pace through the throngs of city workers on their lunch hour until the group around me thins a bit and we speed up, or rather it carries me. Suddenly a gathering of people, a storm of them, me in the middle as if they are protecting me and taking me home without my asking, and I am okay for now in the gray blur of faces and the rough wool of their coats against me, but then I see it, the goal of this crowd, and it is a school, and they are running, not the way a group of people out on their lunch break should approach a school, a school where there are children straining to catch the words of the teacher and maybe, like I was, trying to forget the nights at home and make the picture of the tall tree and the house with smoke curling away off the paper, and the silent but happy dog almost as large as the house.

There is a black man and some children at the top of the stairs, the school doors yawning open, and I think there's nothing unusual in that, but the crowd is screaming and the man pushes the children inside just as some white man from the crowd bursts out of it, and he has plucked the flag from its stand near the entrance and holds it at his side in both hands like a battering ram, though the door to the school is open, completely open, and he can come in if he wants to, even I can, but he is not aiming for the door. He is aiming for the other man with the pointed end of the flagpole, and the crowd is still pushing him and they won't let me turn around. I don't want to see this, I don't want to know if the flagpole's end is so sharp that it can go through the black man's heart, although I think it can, or if it is so strong that it can knock him down under the feet of the crowd, which I'm sure it can. And I am screaming for them to stop but it sounds easily like I am screaming for them to go ahead, but I'm not, although I am there, I am there among them and my hands are empty.

Another white man barrels ahead of the crowd, a short man whose gait is wildly drunk, swinging from one side over to the other, and he rushes up to the black man but does not hit him like the others. He holds something up and the light flashes and I know there will be pictures. His head shines red and bare in the flash of the light, and he is short, much shorter than the others who keep pushing at my back, but then, finally, I am shoved against the wall and fall there, where I stay until someone pulls me inside the school. There I sit and watch the stream of blood fall over my left eye, and tremble like a child at the crimson pooling in my open palm, still in my lap.

I get up to try to leave.

"You okay?" It's the man with the camera.

"I'm not from here. I didn't know what they were going to do. I just walked into this."

"I'm not from here either. Come on, let's get something warm to drink."

He buys me a meal, and I think it's because he wants to, and there's no business transaction involved. We talk about what happened, and we talk about books, and then he drives me to my room and shocks the Madonna by coming inside with me. He fixes up the cut on my forehead, and I fall asleep, waking once or twice to see him there in the chair next to the bed, his camera still and dark on its side. Finally, in the center of night, my eyes open as the door is closing behind him, and it is then that they come, when I am alone again, from Proskurov, from fifty years before this night, to show me the face of my father's fear, to show me the long avenues we are dragged down, tied to the Cossacks' horses. My hair is still, my snakes lie down close to my head, and my mouth is empty, except for the mouth of blood that fills up again over my left eye, as if it has never been tended.

My father, not yet a ghost, is lying down beside me. He catches my eye. I follow him as he rises to go out to

64

the well for water, the bucket swinging into his fourteen year old legs. He knocks the bucket against the fence posts, good strong wood that guides him to water, but then bursts into flame that lights up the neighbor's hair, and then her face, and then her whole fragile bare frame that sinks into the burning earth with her legs spread apart. He runs back to the house without dropping the bucket, and sees them rise from their beds one by one, all grown, somehow, through attack after attack, except for the baby Eli, who hides his face in his mother's skirts. They are all quiet, and so they hear the sound of the horses' hooves receding, and go out, one by one, to see the charred remains, to crouch and whisper into the ear of the girl's mother, who has flung herself to the wet ground beside her, while her father stands in his long underwear and loses his sight. There is no sound, there are no words, and I see my father years later walking through the house at night, or silent for a month at a time when we disobey him.

They are all there, all the ghosts of Proskurov, my thin grandmother Rachel, the one I've never seen, with her wisps of hair not yet white, the lines dark under her eyes, her skirts like an ocean around her. My grandfather's square face, the face on the photo of David, and the girls: Charlotte, Ida, Bessie, Ethel, I know only their Americanized Ellis Island names, and the boys: Frank, Jack, Harry my father, and the baby

Eli. They are all standing around in the small rented room, the ratatat of cough aiming at each one, and I can't make out what they are saying. Others are there, too, murmuring, neighbors and cousins with their own ghosts come to life, the horse with the flesh-covered rope trailing from his rump, the rattle of broken bucket, the well echoing, the water singing as with knowledge, and the ghosts listening, listening to the water and trying to speak to me as I lie there silent, my mouth of blood full, full and wordless, yet.

But I am Devil-Girl, I am a teller of tales, and words will swoon into my heart, spit forth from my broken-toothed mouth, and even my ghosts, my silent ghosts hushed by fire and carried by sea, will speak here. Even stone will agree, even wood will refuse to burn and will shield us, God Almighty, from the riders, who return month after month. There are years when a whole season passes before they come back, when all comes to fruit and is picked from the fields and the trees, when we can buy some of the harvest from the peasants who are allowed to own land. But then, other times, a schoolyard is turned into a field where the bodies are laid, skulls up to the trees, eye sockets alive with darkness, limbs strewn without thought of modesty or jealousy, the ground run red. My father has seen it, and all his family, all the ghosts by my bed have, too, and he has brought the pictures to the

Lower East Side and then to Brooklyn, from the tenements to the projects, and wrapped himself in work and in silence. But I am the Devil's girl, and so I rage against that silence, and he must slap me, again and again, to be quiet as we lie waiting below the line of gunfire, in the root cellar, body upon body, until the hoof beats take another street, another house, another family, another girl.

Then all the ghosts file out, and I am learning to be silent, and each one carries a bag of food and maybe a book or a shirt, and the walk to Warsaw begins for the boat to America, and now I know why, when I step out each morning, I feel as if I have been walking all night, all night long.

I have a typewriter now, and when I wake, I sit, and the rata-tat of the keys answers the cough of the woman next door, and, strangely, quiets it.

That afternoon I walk by the Charles River for hours. Birds are streaming along rivers of clouds, their songs of flight invisible overhead in the shocking winter light, but for sound. I stare into the sun. Song is there.

Swimming

Even now I am not a great swimmer, but, head pushed underwater, a Devil-Kid learns. It's many years since I swam out of the projects, fire still in my eyes, sulfur under my nails, flames at my feet. I swam out with no breath, gasping in the translucence and the mud, kicking with legs that grew as they were pulled apart, into the dream world of crows that humiliated me with their raucous commentary, into the path of speeding subway that left the track to follow me, into the street of boys who barked at me in my deformity, who twisted at my flesh in transformation.

I swam away from the shadow of hands into the hunt that waited for me, into the desert sands of words they punctuated with my names, into the beatings designated for christkillers and niggerlovers and commies and immigrants and the raggedy and the sorry who are beaten by the ones that bore them and the heretics and the landless and the diseased and the witches. I got stuck in the gaping freezer where I slept among the rows of carcasses, where my frozen voice hid between the skinned ribs of soundless history as the walkers passed and slammed the freezer door shut in a pageant of amnesia.

I pried the door open with my cry. I rammed the door open with the bodies of my dreams. I swam up into the hands that lived on top of my head, that lounged in the green world they burned as an occupation. And then I swam up further, through worlds of tangled roots, I swam up with no breath, inhaled mist and fire, and spoke, impossibly, what happened to language, spoke, finally, the journey.

On the Way to School

Breath still down my neck, hot and familiar, the past at my shoulder, the wheels spin beneath me, and I move, by bus, by rail, into the flatlands of farms and bursts of trees. I sway along rivers at dawn, and work through my dreams in the deep night, snacks in my pocket and bag overhead. When I arrive, I am questioned about my hair and my origins. But then I am employed. With an address, and grateful again. Even embraced. I shock some of the local populace, here in the heartland of America, but I work hard at speaking other tongues, at reading small poems to bring gasps and raise respiration in the ice cold nights. I work through the winters, when what is frozen hides my new heart, where warmth now flows through all its chambers, sings at each wall within, makes chorus.

When the hills of snow melt, I stand at the blessed spring, the spring of miracles. The waterfall laughs its loud and roiling spill of power, and I become green again in the summer of the Minnesota plains. And green is everywhere, in graceful arcs above the solid streets, there at my window, caressing the river banks, moving everywhere in the rise of the wind.

Drumming from the center of the earth, from its heart, moves my own to go on.

I hear the call of the loon, but it is the music of millions that pulls me again. The sweet horn that lingers as the subway doors slide shut. The languages that multiply beyond the song of the one tree that lives in my yard. The street corner song. The visible map of society's plan. And I am green again, to feed and to be fed. Ready for strong street shoes, for the tough comeback, for the stray smile. Ready for the music of the world at the crossroads of the subway, in its plunge to tunnel and its arc to bridge. The Salvadoran women praying their way home after the long shift stitching shirts. The Hassid swaying over his Bible, the black child cooing between mother and brother, the girls and their bookbags swinging from the hand straps. The man from Ivory Coast robed and silent. The Italian girl and her mother in discussion, leaning in close. The woman in her jeans humming an aria. The conductor joking between static. The sudden darkness and the suspended breath and the light that follows as the car groans around the curve in the track. O God of iron. O Goddess of journey and safe home.

I decide to return to New York to continue my new life of eating regularly, but I am still so hungry that I try to hide my Devil nature and find a counter to feed at. I am crazy with the flurry of tales of the worlds I already have journeyed. I am hard-pressed to speak, to ask for a sandwich, a drop of drink.

I have been strung to the bed, the posts stretching me to cover the long terrain beneath. I have been poked and gnawed upon, bells of the ceremony lodged in my ear to make tremble all that lives within the cave of skull. Unknown beings have worked their rituals, dreaming their weaponry into me, until I wanted them to, until I wept with the wanting, until I was left shorn of name, and called that which would answer them every time. The fraying of the ropes was accomplished only after what was centuries, unbearable eons, attempted murder.

So I aim to re-enter this world where we walk and talk through the world of school. I fill out applications like I used to tale the johns. Leaving out the dreary; peopling the drama. Telling of work so rough it rises from the page. I fill in the blanks with juice, juice so sweet the committee reads my submission with their tongues. Then, grand lies of omission, of excluded nightmares, of the use of me.

And I am admitted. With rope burns. Hunger pangs. Suffocation. Called upon in class to give answers which would be the reconfiguration of speech. Coming back into this world after traveling other worlds. Bringing back a shoe with a broken heel. A soiled cloth. Skin marked like paper. Skull of rotten fruit. A crushed windpipe. A silent song.

But here I have no words. No words I can write. I have the long-running rant, the pleading, the rage, the repeat repeat of villainy, the violent agreement, the weeping throat, as I look out over the children of the city and see it rolling, gray unstoppable film, violent sputtering hunger.

I do have paper. Electric typewriter. Front bedroom cot. Light bulb. Street noise. Trashcans of the homeless. Silent radiator. Gloves. Lives incised in the walls. Mice search. Roach run. Hard blue drip. Old welts. Older shame.

In class, they think me a footnote. Then off to the bars to pin down the mysteries as I go off to the law firm to read contracts and wills and depositions for a twelve hour shift, and expunge a comma, correct a misspelling, bracket a passage the opposing lawyer has slipped in without mentioning. Through the night the film keeps unrolling, unstoppable by silence, and in the morning I write, with the pounding of my heart, of the maimed faces and the cry always crouched here, within me.

I will learn to write. I am silent and tongue-tied, strangled and barely breathing, but I will learn to write and to speak, there, at the university.

What delusion! What truth! What twisted rubble of the heart after so many death threats after so many stabbings after the dream of chorus and not the marching images of power, not the airy golf green and the welcoming split-level and the momentary rough cloth of the students from the suburbs come to the city and walking gingerly past the displaced. O cries in the hallways of the beaten child! O longing to return of the drunk fallen in the streets! O trembling at the broken window of the junky! O rage of the vet, rape of the daughters, lost bus careening into the wall, bleeding blades of grass, sunflowers lost in the razed streets, night games of children! O the holy hell of this city for the unprotected! O my wounds! My silence. My shame.

But I am safe on 90th Street with Addie, a blessing of home and hot meals, a woman delicate and strong, her wisps of gray hair flying always into the light. She asks me, "How was school last night?" as my eyes, burning with all-night work, squint at her.

"They thought that a poem about a suburban father's golf game touched on universal themes, but my poem about immigrants could only include lines about Dominicans if there were footnotes, footnotes about the invasion of Santo Domingo. Hundreds of thousands of Domicanos in New York and they think everyone who speaks Spanish here is Puerto Rican."

"Eat some pot roast before you go in," and Addie heaps my plate with the meat that falls shredded into its own juices, and potatoes red with paprika, sweet carrots, and long green beans. I am grateful, and look down into the meal before me, inhale the aroma, and jump up to hug her thin shoulders as she waves me off and imperiously points me back to my chair. "You need food that sticks to you. Other people's blindness always makes me hungry."

So I eat. She pushes me out the door when I finish, though I protest leaving the leftovers unwrapped and the dirty dishes still on the table. She enters my heart forever, and makes me figure out I can do this, somehow, complete this adventure in education.

Here in school. Given the homework of writing. Bring in the poem. Bring the story. Devil-Girl graded on truth. Lose points as I have lost memory.

As I have lost memories. For this I write. To remember. To make the story of my life. To hear the others speaking in me and through me. To open the rough stitched cross of autopsy and let spill the truth forgotten there, let it be read for the future.

I must leave my Addie, my haven, my glimpse of safety. She is ill and my room must go to the live-in nurse. Addie's sorry, for us both, I think. Her phonebook fills with each new address and phone number for me, in her large unsteady handwriting. I try to hold on to her voice. I call. "And how are *you*?" she demands as answer to each of my questions about her health. I don't tell her how much I miss her.

I am still a student. Notebooks. Textbooks. Questions. Answers. The rain beating against the roof of the classroom. The air around me thick as gauze.

Nodding from sleeplessness. Eyes burning. Heart pounding. Adrenals pumping. Poem a cry.

Barely breathing for two years, then granted a degree. Paper. Thin paper still. But what can open my mouth? What can blur my shame? What can forgive my silence? What can use me well? Use my disasters?

This. The holy word. Word of those judged devil. This grunt of pain. This recognition. All the children, calling to be seen.

Education, or Getting Into the Pictures

As Devil-Girl, I've lived with the gangs of children that run about the planet, the ones they call criminals and wolves and whores and sluts and brats and lazy ones, the ones who are fat and skinny and ugly and marked, yes, the ones who are marked, their skin pitted, one eye wandering, their teeth rotten, their voices cracking, or hoarse, or whispered behind their palms. I've lived also with the beauty of children, what it aches to look at, and I've hidden under the bed when their beauty, so unbearable, was taken. I've stood before the hung children, the sorrow of trees. I've seen them cooked raw in scalding water; I've seen them devoured. I've seen their bellies swell with hunger, and I know that the ones they call bad are the ones who are filled with the emptiness of the planet.

How do I know this? Don't make me laugh. Look into it yourself. Don't ask me for seventy cents a day to save the children. Instead, stop bombing them. Stop destroying the pipes that bring them clean water so they have to drink what's filled with the bacteria that runs through them, and empties them of strength and life. Don't destroy their crops, kill their animals, erode their land, bomb their fishermen, and then charge them interest for the privilege. This is not complicated. This is elementary education. Show me I'm wrong, but, remember, my sight was forged in the factory of nightmares, in the city dump of children, in the scourge of the family, in the iron maiden of history, in the myth of once upon a time and believe me I know it was not once, not an accident, not an isolated individual acting alone. Remember, I was spit out by a taxi into the middle of a city falling down since the first slave entered here and the first Indian was murdered and the first child was called demon and thrown to the boot of the beefy well-fed, well-dressed pretenders to the throne of it all, this flat unyielding world of maps, of boundaries, of the colonial hand.

Well, the joke's on me. Though school has been a torment, a warehouse of the unspoken, I stay. Now, school becomes a home; books, food; and the students my own Devil-Children. The further they are thrown, out of the family or out of the last school or into jail or out of the shelter, the more they are knocked around, the more my hair stands up and wraps them in adoring waves.

O children, I am with you, though they may tear down brick by brick each place where I plant my Devil-seeds and toss books at you like candy, try to fill your emptiness with words and pictures of your own beauty and the long gentle boats that could carry you off to home each night, to the fire of community and the feast of what the centuries have gathered.

This school where I have come to teach is full of voices, all kinds of voices, and they warm me. Each year I take photographs of my students to give them back a hint of their beauty. They love to pose, in big groups with their arms outstretched and me in the center grinning foolishly, or in coiled couples, or each one alone, filling up the whole frame of the camera's eye. I finally appear when the film is developed, after decades of never turning up in photos, no matter how the shutter clicked furiously, no matter who similarly appeared there in the negatives.

Now I am surrounded by the angels called devils of the late twentieth century, the children dropped out, so clearly my own, my family. They call me Mother, they call me Sister, they call me Girl for short and leave out the Devil. They have been told so often that their English is "broken", but to my mind, now beginning to dance, broken English is only that which has been battered into silence, humiliated into stopping, never saying what you mean, never asking for what you want, eyes broken off from the words that find air. So we do a lot of work on different kinds of Englishes—we read the Black English of Toni Morrison's Pecola in *The Bluest Eye* on falling in love, and then *Romeo and Juliet*'s "What light from yonder window breaks..."; we translate Bob Marley's insistent "Dem belly full but we 'ungry..." into Standard American English; we eat up the prose of Latino writers like Piri Thomas, Nicholasa Mohr, Pedro Juan Soto, about Spanish Harlem. I read Yiddish-American stories to them in the best accent of my past, and they like the questioning music and wild, insistent logic of those voices. They learn their essay exam, job interview and college English, and still cherish and feed their own Englishes that galvanize the listeners whose ears they dance into.

But it isn't easy, this bilingualism, or, for some of the Spanish- and Creole- and Chinese-speakers, trilingualism. One day, three of my students, Justine, Inez and Cassandra, stay after class to talk about their frustrations. Inez didn't do so well on the last exam and begins to cry. She needs her diploma and a job. She has to get out of her mother's house. Her mother's boyfriend keeps putting his hands on her. She says, Next time, I'll kill him. Cassandra holds her and we all sit close and whisper to her. She agrees to take on extra work to push up her scores, and to tell her mother what's been going on right under her nose. I stroke Inez's face and wipe her tears, joke with her until she breaks out into a smile that washes the room with light. Justine in her beautiful hard face keeps back, holding Inez's hand but not looking at her.

That night I study my collection of photographs. I stop at the few I have of Justine, and spread them out on the rug in a small circle of light. In each one she wears her shades, her mouth drawn tightly or puckered self-consciously. She pushes at the air with her breasts, juts her hips out, caresses her shoulders above crossed arms and barely looks out from beneath heavy lids.

Many young men at school are after Justine. She talks hard at them, calls them over and pushes them away. She always does her homework, handing in pages of assignments, beautifully done. She has just turned seventeen, and says she is finished with the streets. But when I ask the class to write about a memory they can't forget, something that keeps returning to their minds, she hands in nothing.

She comes back to see me after class, the day that assignment is due, Inez and Cassandra with her as ever.

We all sit on the desks in the back, our legs dangling like children's. Inez says it's better at home now, he's leaving her be. He came up behind her when she was studying, but she'd hidden a knife underneath her book and pointed it straight at his heart before he could get too close. That seems to have settled the matter.

Cassandra wants to talk about her date. It's the first time she's ever been out with a white man, and it was alright, she says, except when the news came on his car radio to remind her that it was the anniversary of Yusef's murder at the hands of white thugs in

Bensonhurst. Then she peered over at him, at his sharp nose and the pale glow of his face, and wondered whether what she was doing was a betrayal, a betrayal of Yusef's memory, a repeat of history, a slap in the face of her own. But then he held her hand, without a word, and she could feel something pass between them that was the same in both of them.

She is going through the details, where they ate and what, how she had imagined what it would be like to kiss his mouth, a mouth so different from her own, when Justine begins to speak, staring straight out and tapping her foot against the rung of the desk.

"It don't matter to me," she says, "what color they are. They either treat you bad or they treat you good. And you got to be ready for it, no matter what it is. One time, I wasn't. I was thirteen, or maybe just fourteen, and I was late, like I always was, for school. I was thinking maybe not to go that day, but I decided I would, and I was at the bus stop walking up and back to pass the time until the bus came. This really fly car stopped, and the music was pumped up, you know, saying, 'Justine, forget about that old ninth grade today.' There was two black guys and a white guy inside, and they looked okay and asked if they could give me a lift. I thought I really should try to get to school, so I told them where the school was at, and they was all polite and I was, too, thanking them and everything for the lift, talking 'bout how slow that old bus was, 'specially when you late.

"I sat back for a while and chilled, then I looked up expecting that we was real close, but I see we going across the bridge into Jersey, and the wind be blowing real hard and I'm shouting against the wind that it's the wrong way. The guy driving tell me, don't worry, we just making a quick stop. I guess I started to worry then, and held real tight to my looseleaf.

"Well, we made a stop, but it wasn't no quick one. They kept me for hours, they did it to me for hours, and I thought I wasn't never getting out alive. It was real quiet there, some town out in Jersey — I never did know which town it was, but it seemed like all the people around was dead, there wasn't nobody to hear me, and I gave up screaming after they started knocking me around. All I could hear was the bass of the radio and the sounds they made doing it to me, or yelling at each other to do it to me more."

She stops, and we all stay quiet, barely breathing. She keeps staring, and after a while says, "I never told nobody that before. Nobody ever gonna hurt me like that again."

I see Inez clench her fist. Cassandra whispers, "That's right, girl. Nobody."

Then I tell her things, more things than I have ever told a student before, more than I would tell the other teachers. The next day she hands in two pages for the assignment she missed on a memory. She tells of almost skipping school, and her ride to Jersey in the wind over the strange song of the bridge, how a white man was riding about with black men, and how quiet the town was. She tells of staring at the red glow of the radio dial, of listening to the low voices of men, and of the silent ride back into Manhattan. She never speaks of hands and force, she never mentions what it was they did to her. But everyone who reads it, knows.

Hurricane, or A Family Visit

Now I wheel her outside into the moist sunlight, into the fans of palm trees, with the scraping of wheels on the concrete ramp like the old roller skate song down the hills of East New York, and I try to be gentle. And, later that night, I will try to be more than gentle as I turn her from side to side and swab the sores that eat her up, morsel of age, because she refuses to get out of bed anymore.

All afternoon I see the sunlight gleam silver in the one child braid that juts forth from the back of her neck, and she calls out from time to time as if she is in danger of falling, but I cup her hand in mine and whisper that she is fine, and that I won't let her go. There is nothing else to do. Nothing else to think. Rage is wordless now, inhaling the disinfectant and softening in the glow of the television which is always on, low and garbled. There is nothing else to say, but, here is your juice, can you eat a little more cereal? Are you warm enough?

As she sleeps, I light a candle and watch it burn down, running soft veins of heat away from the dancing flame. She would never have a true fire in her home, and me, I can't live without one. She wakes up from her nap cursing me, her Devil-Child, pointing into my face, saying that I've stolen all her money and eaten all her food, and I say, no, that's not so, and walk away for a while, stare out the picture window as the rising air stirs the trees and pulls at the hair of a woman passing by with her shopping cart behind her like a toy wagon.

When she is calmer, she mumbles, sorry, sorry, and I roll her chair over to the terrace so that she can watch the wind also. She peers up into the blue, her hand shading her eyes.

I watch her day and night, and chat with the nurse who comes to check her. When a friend comes by to insist on driving me out to the ocean, I am ready for it, needing to stand where I can see beyond the apartment, further than the ceiling where God lives and observes us each moment, where the waves roar louder than the curses in old Yiddish, and the sun burns brighter than the yellow flowers on the Melmac plates that gape open still, as they did when I was small. I am ready to walk along the water, to crouch in the sand and watch the work of tides, the stealing away and the return of things that never seemed to belong to earth, to the shore, to us.

I have been frightened of water for so long, frightened of losing my breath in the world beneath the surface, but my friend insists I practice putting my head down under the waves. My mother's breath is slowing down, my mother is going under the surface of the blue night, and, as I bring myself under, I can see another world, where all is grace, where I can stay under or bring myself back through the edge into the world of air, of wind, of howl, of song, and I decide to leave her, her hair blue and dancing with the waves, her body healed in the salt water and the earth's heat, her arms reaching behind her, her mouth empty.

There has been a hurricane lately, and the tangle of remains lingers at the shoreline. We step through it, ocean water and sweat streaming over our skin. All that lies there is eaten by salt and the force of the water, by rocks and by wind. All that remains is its own language; nothing the way it was before the storm. We are lucky to travel these worlds and live.

Tonight on the news, there is the story of a boy who is sent from his village in Honduras on an errand. He is able to return only after the hurricane has flooded his town, and all, all, everything is under the water, everyone is gone. The camera points down at him as he tosses on one of the cots set up for the area's survivors. *"Solo yo,"* he cries, over and over again, *"solo yo."* Only me, he says, as his whole village, his whole family, is finally swallowed into the silence of the receding waters, the new calm.

I leave the set on and go to watch her, and for hours, until just before the light, the time between her breaths lengthens, as in her rages it shortened. I think about Zeno, was it? about how the distance between two points can be cut in half an infinite number of times, how no one will ever reach the other side of one's step according to this theory, but at 5:10 in the morning, my mother proves him wrong, and reaches the end of her breath, stops calling out to those who are dead, and goes to the other side. *Solo yo*, I think, as I watch the pain leave her and the stillness settle in. *Solo yo*.

Devil-Children

Karla Faye Tucker in a drug-induced craze brutally took human life, orgiastically, orgasmically slaughtered, but now she has found God in prison. Even the relatives of her victims trust her conversion, her transformation, and though she will be executed, electric current the scourge of every cell in her completely Christian body, she is forgiven. God loves her, her minister has become her husband, and though white and a woman, she still fits the bill for execution coming from a poor working family, and so the anti-death penalty forces love her. And I love her, I love her as the one who will die for the sins I might have committed. I love her for the rage that lifted her hands to murder while it only left me spinning in silence, me at the center of the target, killing no one, at least none that I can remember, though, like many, I came close to killing my furious self.

So am I, Karla Faye's true sister, still the bull's-eye for blame, and the bull's-eye for violence? Or is it four-year old Woodcaby Dieujuste, taken from his family in Haiti to serve another family as slave, laboring in the household from six in the morning till ten o'clock at night? Is he the mascot of the Just God, his smile infectious, his willing hands doing the work as grown men and women lounge on couches in the heat? I was the nightmare girl, colorless, slipping away into a stain on the bed, hair a fright, crackling with electricity, stomach aching into the night, bones stretched too long on the old bed of the masters. I was a cursed child, the one whose forebears had been devoured and who only now come by from time to time to see how I eat, what I am reading, and whether I dream.

I am a refugee from dead towns, joined in blood with the other children who watch their villages sinking under the weight of centuries. And with this joining, the stories hum, the stories raise themselves to the glory of chorus, and stories turn humiliation to ash.

Now I can sit down. Now I can remember. Now I can make the words to tell.

Greeting the Millennium with Devil-Girl

They tried exorcism, couldn't beat the Devil out of me; excavation, to find my true obedience; extermination, I wouldn't die.

They settled on excommunication, expulsion, but I am still here, and my stories make them mad. Now the invisible dead and their reborn magic hands hold me up over the chasm of earth's center and fly with me through the night.

I am Devil-Girl. I weep and cry out all the beatings and the takings. I exhume the bodies, explain the exact cause of death. I excrete the poisons, explode the time bombs, exhale the breath of death-in-life. I inhale the wild spirits and magical moons that throb like my own body.

I was the one who waited in the womb for the right moment, waited for September first to be born, saving up all that ache and sway, that howl and ride, the Devil song, that dance of hips and let go words, that open up mouth and those visions. I waited decades more, to simply tell. Now, I still weep for others, but I sing for them, too, little Devil-Girl, going home.

It is now the twenty-first century. Many years of drinking Devil-juice have passed. I am immune to Marlon B and his motorcycle sneer, to undershirts and the charm of convertibles. I am free from failing grades and untrue hands, from puppet masters and saviors. I am unfazed by a harsh word, by a slap, by an order. Immune to the long thigh and the deadly whisper, the locked school and the pampered babble. I am immune to memory. I am immune to the loss of memory. I am immune to breakdown and to curse. I am full of prayer and moonlight, scars and the wild birth of new skin. I am full of belief in air, full of the sandwich of dawn and dusk, the green mist that breathes with me, the joy of hands, the mouth's knowledge, the belly's song.

I climb the rocks to the burial ground of fear. After a while, I wipe my hands of the good dirt I have flung there. I am swooning into the possibility of the end of the world, each atom moving away from the other into endlessness and the inside of song. I remember sobbing between the missiles aimed at us and the missiles we aimed, and dreaming the world under the desk, the ride beneath the earth, the journey into spring. I remember the green love for the mystery that lived beneath the beard of warning of the midtown prophet crushed between the towers of stone, the crowds of wallets, the jeers of perfumes. I loved his rigid refusal to slip out of sight, to give in. I want to know this being who is a wooden card and a god in one, a living prophecy of the fate of the world. I want the revelations he holds. I want to drink with him in upside down splendor. I want to know whether the bombs lodged among the red hills and juniper trees are only the dream of the sandwich man, or if they are truly the language of the millennium. They are definitely no joke.

I want to know the whimper of their power taken down.

I want to know how to hold them, as their creators have held us hostage since the first desert shock of bomb, a test of our blindness.

I've followed the wooden man all the way here to the place of the cottonwoods, a silent place except for the hum of missiles rushing down the production belt near the silent shuddering volcano of the grand valley, where the elk have come out to look at me. I want to decipher the message of the missiles, and for this I will live and live beyond the natural lifespan of a Devil-child, and slowly, slowly, breathe in the darkness, and bare my sharp teeth, up to the bone.

Laugh if you want to. But this is the language of the end of the world.

Or not.

Milagrito (Little Miracle)

I have run the length of the planet away from the stories my body tells. I have flown up into sky, into clouds edged with golden light, shafts of rain illuminated, into the indigo hands of slaves opening up the top of the world, washing the blue hills, erupting into rainbows, washing our sight.

My body is miracle. Dagger in the heart, the heart heals. Legs broken, then they run. Membrane ripped jagged, it flowers. The mother I never had giving rays of yellow light, shielding the body and its journey from the precision of lightning, from revenge, from blindness.

Birds in flight, fix these to my body. Eyes of strong vision at the crossing. Books opening. Hands, eyes in the palms, hearts at the junction of life and love, tributaries I ache to wander, all miracle.

All the stories of the body, its exquisite work, wood, leather, silver, the green turquoise eye, the stone of the heart carved by oceans into an impossible and enduring being, speak on in the silence of the hills, in the desert heat, in the dissolution of years of time into space, into earth, into ruin and flower, into the dance of the planet.

Judge these legs strong on the pathway held up by the heat of the earth and the flow of its song. Hear as miracle the echo of footsteps. Count and recount the echoes of miracle, until each one is heard, and each one returns.

Sing, child, sing, you who also journeys.

Notes for *The Stories of Devil-Girl*

Mother and Child:

The *Zohar*, or *Book of Splendor*, the most important work of the Kabbalistic movement, was written about 1286, most likely by Moses de Leon in Castile, Spain.

I use this quote describing Lilith in this terrible way because although this image of Lilith, the one who considered herself Adam's equal and fled or was cast out of the Garden, may have come from men's fear of the feminine and her power, images repeated thus through the ages sometimes gather a kind of reality, find human beings to carry out their work, and must, I feel, be examined in light of both the realities and the projections from which they are constituted.

Prayer:

Tefilin or phylacteries are, according to the Oxford English Dictionary, "a small leathern box containing four texts of Scripture...written in Hebrew letters on vellum and...worn by Jews during morning prayer on all days except the Sabbath, as a reminder of the obligation to keep the law."

They are tied on with leathern thongs.

On the status of women, according to the Talmud, "the summary of oral law that evolved after centuries of scholarly effort by sages who lived in Palestine and

Babylonia until the beginning of the Middle Ages," and is "the central pillar" of Judaism:

"Talmudic law excludes women, in many ways, from several important spheres of life....These include many of the familiar rituals of Jewish life: wearing the *tzitzit* (fringed four-cornered garment), laying *tefilin* (phylacteries), reciting the *Shema Yisrael* prayer, blowing the *shofar*... and pilgrimage. Women are not permitted to join a *minyan* (quorum of ten) for prayer, nor are they assigned active functions within the community. As for their social status, they are not eligible for administrative and judicial positions. And, most significant of all, they are exempt from the most important *mitzvah* (blessing) of studying Torah, a fact that inevitably precludes them from playing a part in Jewish cultural and spiritual life." (Of course, this has changed in many congregations.)

Adin Steinsaltz's *The Essential Talmud*, Basic Books, Inc., New York, 1976, pages 3-4, 137.

Marriage Rituals:

Part of the ceremony of marriage under Judaism has been described this way:

"The rabbi recites the seven wedding benedictions (*sheva berakhot*) over a glass of wine. The bride and the groom drink from the glass, then the groom smashes it with his foot. A variety of interpretations are given for this ancient custom. Most historians agree that it must have originated with the desire to drive away evil spirits....The rabbinic interpretation is that in the midst of gladness we always recall our sorrows, and that we break the glass to remember the destruction of the Temple."

Arlene Rossen Cardozo's *Jewish Family Celebrations: The Sabbath, Festival, and Ceremonies*, St. Martin's Press, New York, 1982, page 222.

Milagrito (Little Miracle):

Milagrito means "little miracle" in Spanish. The word refers here to the practice in the Southwest and in Latin America of hammering small silver objects into a cross which is offered, with prayers, to the saints. The objects on the *milagrito* correspond to aspects of life with which the supplicant needs help.

The last line is a variation on a line by Charles Olson, from *The Maximus Poems*, Jargon/Corinth Books, New York, 1960; "The Songs of Maximus", Song 6, page 16:

> "you sing, you
> who also
> wants."

About the Author

Anya Achtenberg is an award-winning fiction writer and poet. Her recently completed novel, *More Than The Wind*, was excerpted in *Harvard Review*. Her second book of poetry, *The Stone of Language*, was published in 2004 by *West End Press*. Her stories have received awards from Coppola's *Zoetrope: All-Story*, *New Letters*, the Asheville Fiction Writers Workshop, the Raymond Carver Story Contest and others. She received a 2008 Minnesota State Arts Board Grant for work on *History Artist*, a novel-in-progress, centering on Devi Mau, a Cambodian woman born of an African-American father at the moment the bombing of Cambodia began. She is working on a book to turn her multi-genre course, *Writing for Social Change: Re-Dream a Just World*, into a moveable workshop.

She has taught creative writing at universities and colleges, for writers' organizations, with drop-out youth, working adults, and in the public schools. She teaches independent workshops throughout the country and online, on essential elements of story in fiction and memoir; deepening characterization; autobiography and autobiographical fiction; and writing for social change. She offers manuscript consultations in fiction, poetry, and memoir.

Visit her website *Writing Story / Finding Poetry / Freeing Voice: Swimming through the ocean of language* at www.AnyaAchtenberg.com

www.ingramcontent.com/pod-product-compliance
Lightning Source LLC
Chambersburg PA
CBHW050308260626
47156CB00005B/1708